Get that Ghost
to Go Too!

by

Catherine MacPhail

Illustrated by Karen Donnelly

You do not need to read this page –
just get on with the book!

First published in 2006 in Great Britain by
Barrington Stoke Ltd
www.barringtonstoke.co.uk

ISBN-10: 1-842993-73-9
ISBN-13: 978-1-84299-373-6

Printed in Great Britain by Bell & Bain Ltd

MEET THE AUTHOR – CATHERINE MACPHAIL

What is your favourite animal?
Elephant
What is your favourite boy's name?
David
What is your favourite girl's name?
Sarah
What is your favourite food?
Prawns
What is your favourite music?
Dean Martin singing
That's Amore
What is your favourite hobby?
Writing

MEET THE ILLUSTRATOR – KAREN DONNELLY

What is your favourite animal?
Woodlice!
What is your favourite boy's name?
Laurie
What is your favourite girl's name?
Jean
What is your favourite food?
Sausages and runny eggs
What is your favourite music?
Beck
What is your favourite hobby?
Drawing and printmaking

For my own little
Ross,

Ross William Cherry

Contents

Chapter 1
Dean's Back

I remember everything that happened so well. From the moment the nightmare began all over again.

School was over for the day and I was sitting in the café with Greg and Markie. I'm Duncan, by the way. Greg, Markie and Ross are my best mates. That afternoon we were all waiting for Ross to arrive. "What's taking him so long?" I said.

Just then Ross came in the door. As always he had his dogs with him. He just loves his dogs. His face was all scratched and bleeding. He looked like something out of a horror film.

"What happened to you?" Markie asked.

"I bet it was Dean who did that," Greg said. Greg was clever. He was the cleverest boy in the school. He knew everything.

Yes, it had to be Dean. Dean was a cat who had been a ghost once. A bad ghost. The ghost of a teddy boy. He'd had ginger hair. One of his eyes was green, the other one was blue. We had got rid of him with a magic rap song. But Dean had come back. Not as a ghost, but as a ginger cat.

Now he lived with Ross and his family of stray dogs but he still made everyone's life a misery. He was always scratching Ross, or leaving cat hair all over the sofas. Sometimes he spat up fur balls into Ross's dinner or did his poos in the worst places, like in the middle of the carpet or on Ross's bed.

Ross rubbed his face. "He won't scratch me again," he said. "He's run away."

"Good riddance," I said. "Let's hope that's the last we see of him."

"Oh, I think we'll still see him, Duncan," Ross told me. "He didn't go too far, he just moved in next door."

Markie was sitting next to me. He sat up quickly. "Next door?" he said. He sounded shocked.

"Next door to your house?" Greg asked, just as shocked.

"Next door ... to your house ... where the witch lives?" I asked. I was beginning to shake.

Ross laughed. "Baggie Maggie's not a witch," he said. "She's just a bit dotty."

Baggie Maggie, the daft old bat who lived next door to Ross, was more than a bit dotty. She wandered about the town collecting bags. Bin bags, plastic bags, paper bags, handbags, nappy bags. Whatever sort of bag you can think of, Baggie Maggie collected it. She always had a bag on her head as a hat. That woman just loved bags. Baggie Maggie told everyone that she was a witch. She was always putting spells on people.

"Her spells don't work," Ross said. "It's not her fault that awful things happen to people she doesn't like. It's just bad luck."

Ross could never see anything bad in anyone. He had to be the kindest person you could ever meet.

"So has Dean gone to live with Baggie Maggie? Next door to you?" Markie asked.

"Baggie Maggie always liked him. She puts out milk, and things for him to eat, like fish heads and dead mice and stuff."

"Every witch needs a cat," Greg said, softly. I told you, Greg's really clever.

"She's not a witch," Ross insisted.

"I think we'll have to check this out. Follow me," Markie said. He was bold. He was the bravest boy in the school, scared of nothing. I know, because he told me.

So we all ran with Markie to Baggie Maggie's house. Her garden was like a jungle, and she had plastic bags tied round her bushes. Instead of flowers she had bags on sticks all over her garden. They were all the colours of the rainbow. Blue bags and red bags and purple bags and green bags. She said she was trying to grow them, that bags were the loveliest flowers in the world.

This woman's lift did not go to the top floor, Greg always said.

All of a sudden a weird noise filled the air.

I put my hands over my ears. "What's that?" The sound was like nails being scratched down a blackboard.

"I think Maggie's singing," Ross said.

"Who told her she could sing?" Markie asked. He stuffed two hankies in his ears.

"That can't be singing!" I said, and listened. "It sounds as if she's being tortured – horribly."

"Don't let Baggie Maggie hear you say that," Greg said. "Colin Morris said something rude about her singing once and look what happened to him."

"You mean ... cross-eyed Colin?" We all knew Colin. He was the only boy in school who could look two ways at once.

Markie nodded. "He wasn't cross-eyed before he insulted Maggie."

We followed the terrible sound of her singing round the path behind her house. The kitchen window was open and Baggie Maggie was making the dinner. She was wearing a party bag on her head. It was covered with stars and read,

CONGRATULATIONS ON THE NEW BABY

She also had a plastic bag tied round her waist. This one said,

THANK YOU FOR SHOPPING AT TESCO

A black bin bag was pinned round her shoulders like a cloak. She was stirring a bubbling pot on the hob.

"Toad's eyes and rat's tails," Markie whispered. "I heard that's all she eats."

Just then she picked up something long and thin that looked just like a rat's tail. She held it in her fingers above her mouth and dropped it in. "Perfect!" she said with a chuckle.

Markie nearly fainted. "She's gross," he said. "I'm sure that was a rat's tail."

"It was spaghetti," Ross said.

"It was brown, Ross," I told him.

"Well, it was brown spaghetti," Ross said.

Just then, Baggie Maggie called out. "Dinner, darling Dean, come to Mummy."

"She's calling for the cat," Ross said. We all peered through the window so we could see Dean, the evil ginger cat, with one green eye and one blue, pad into her kitchen for his dinner.

But it wasn't a cat who came into the kitchen. It was a teddy boy with ginger hair. His hair was swept up into a wave you could have surfed on. He was wearing tight trousers that looked like drainpipes and black winkle picker shoes with long pointy toes. He had one green eye, and one blue.

It was Dean. And he was back.

Chapter 2
Call Me Mum

"Is that really Dean?" Ross asked.

Markie stumbled. He was ready to pass out. "Tell me I'm seeing things."

Greg didn't understand. "But how come we can see him now?"

It was Dean all right. Before, I had been the only one who could see him, with his one green eye and the other one blue. Now, he was back and we could all see him. How could that be?

We didn't have to wait long for an answer. Baggie Maggie ruffled Dean's hair. "Those bad boys turned you into a cat, son. And we can't have that. I've turned you back into a boy again. You're the son I never had."

She'd done it. Baggie Maggie had changed Dean from a cat back into a boy and this time we could all see him.

Baggie Maggie emptied the whole bubbling pot onto Dean's plate. It still looked like rats' tails to me. They squirmed on his plate as if they were alive. Then she dumped a couple of sausages on top of it all.

"It's wonderful to be able to eat again, Maggie," Dean said.

Maggie smiled at him. Lots of her teeth were missing. "Call me Mum."

Dean looked at her and grinned. Half a sausage stuck out of his mouth like a big fat worm. "Mum," he mumbled.

I'm pretty sure I could see a tear glint in Baggie Maggie's eyes. "Eat up your sausages, son," she said. "I've got a nice plate of apple pie and custard for your pudding."

"Yum, yum, yum, Mum," Dean said and he got stuck into the sausages.

We all hid down under the window.

"Maybe he's forgotten all about us," Ross said.

"Yes, he'll be quite happy here with Baggie Maggie," Greg said. "We don't need to worry."

"I'm sure he won't hold a grudge," Markie muttered. "He won't remember how we got rid of him."

I knew better. Last time Dean was around I'd been the only one who could see him. I'd seen his nasty smile and I remembered what he'd said. "I'll be back," he'd promised. And now he was. I was sure he'd want revenge.

We peeked into the kitchen again just as Baggie Maggie gave Dean his apple pie. It was covered in custard and the custard had loads of lumps in it. They looked like boils ready to burst. I wouldn't have eaten that if you'd paid me.

"There you are, son," she said.

"Thanks, Mum," Dean simpered. He sounded so sweet and grateful.

"Maybe Baggie Maggie's spell changed him," Markie whispered to me. "He seems quite nice now."

We watched as Dean almost ate the plate as well as the pie. "This is wonderful. I can eat again. I never want to munch into a dead mouse again." He gave Maggie a big smile. "And it's all thanks to you, Mum."

"I'd do anything for you, son," Baggie Maggie said.

"Tell me, can everyone see me now?" Dean asked her.

Baggie Maggie shook her head. "No, dear. Just me, and those bad boys that turned you into a cat." She said it as if she hated those "bad boys".

Greg's hair stood on end. We all held our breath.

"That wasn't a nice thing to do, was it, Mum?" Dean said.

Baggie Maggie began to get angry. "No, it was not. It was a bad, bad thing. But let me tell you, son ..."

Now she started to wave her finger about as if it was Darth Vader's lightsaber. "Just you say the word, and I'll make those boys really sorry."

"Will you, Mum?" Dean asked her.

Maggie came across and patted Dean's head. "Oh yes, darling. I have ways of making them very sorry for what they did to you."

"Great," Dean said. Then he turned his face to the window so fast we didn't have time to duck down and hide. I think he knew we were there from the beginning. He grinned at us in that nasty way I knew so well. "Great," he said again. "I want you to make them really sorry. Now!"

Chapter 3
I Can't See You!

I've never been so scared in all my life. Dean was back, and he was coming after us. And now he even had a witch to help him.

We were doomed.

"She's not a witch," Ross kept saying.

But everyone knew bad things happened to the people she didn't like.

And now, she didn't like us.

"There's only one thing for it," Greg said. His hair was still standing on end.

"We'll have to go somewhere far away," Markie said. "I'll go and get my passport." He was ready to run.

I was ready to run too. "We'll hide," I said. "I know the perfect place. Timbuctoo. In the middle of nowhere."

"No." Greg dragged us back. "We can't run away. We got rid of Dean once. We'll get rid of him again."

I remembered the trouble we'd had the last time. All of us dancing around and chanting, "Get that Ghost to Go".

And we'd done it too. We had got rid of him, but not for long.

"So do we do the chant again?" I said.

Greg shook his head. "No. It won't work twice. No. I'll have to think about it." He walked off deep in thought. If anyone could save us, it was Greg. His brilliant brain would work something out. He would stay up all night and spend hours on the Internet until he found the answer.

Until then, we were in trouble.

Next day at school Greg told us what we had to do.

"We ignore him," he said. "Act as if he isn't there. It will get right up his nose if we pretend we can't see him."

"You're sure this will work?" Markie asked him.

"I don't know," Greg had to admit. "But it's worth a try."

He was right, as always. We couldn't think of anything else we could do, so we tried it. We were going to ignore Dean, pretend he wasn't there.

Our first chance came later that day when we were going home after school. We looked across the playground and there was Dean, as large as life. He was leaning against the school gates. He stared over at us and gave a nasty grin. Everyone else was running about, darting past him, just as if he wasn't there.

"Can't anyone else see him?" Markie asked.

"No," I said. "Remember what Baggie Maggie said. We're the only ones who can see him."

"He looks just like a real flesh and blood boy to me," Markie said. "The kind you could punch in the face. Want me to try it?"

He looked at me. There was no one as bold as Markie, scared of nothing. I know because he told me.

I wanted to let him, but I remembered what Greg had said. We had to pretend Dean wasn't there.

The three of us walked slowly towards Dean. It was as if we didn't see him. Greg started reading a book. Markie looked inside his rucksack. And I stared at the sky.

Dean stopped leaning on the gates in front of us. He started walking beside us. "Going somewhere?" he asked with a snarl.

"Think it will rain?" I said, holding out my hand as if I could feel it already.

Greg kept reading his book. "This is brilliant," he said. "I can't put it down."

Markie pretended he had lost something. "Has anyone seen my comic?" he said.

Dean waved his hands about. "I'm here! I'm back!" he shouted. But we still ignored him.

"I'm here!" he yelled. He stuck out his foot and Markie tripped over it. He fell face down in a puddle.

Dean laughed.

"Wake up, Markie, you aren't looking where you're going," I said, as I helped him to his feet.

"Yeah." Markie got up. "Silly me."

Dean began to get angry. "You *can* see me, I know you can!" With that he punched Greg right on the nose. Blood spurted all over the ground. Greg fell back. "Oh, dear, another of my nosebleeds. I get them all the time." He said it very softly. I was most impressed.

Dean was getting madder by the minute. "That was me! That was me! I did it!"

But we all ignored him. Greg was right. Dean didn't like that at all. He jumped up and down and pulled at his hair. "It was me!"

Markie helped Greg up. I gave him a hankie to stop the blood. "Come on, Greg," I said. "We'll go and get something to stop that nosebleed."

We walked right past Dean as if he wasn't there. As he watched us, he scratched his head. "That daft old woman," he moaned. "She's done something wrong. They can't see me at all."

Then he grinned. "But I've still got Ross."

Chapter 4
Good Game!

Ross! We all ran as fast as we could to Ross's house. Ross would never be able to pretend he couldn't see Dean. Ross can't tell a lie. Can you believe that? He has never ever told a lie. But this time, he had to. Our lives depended on it.

Ross was in his garden playing with his dogs when we got there. We couldn't see Dean anywhere.

"Ross," I said, "when Dean comes here you have to pretend you can't see him."

"Pretend?" I could tell he hardly understood what the word meant. "Do you mean like ... lie?"

Greg tried to explain. "It's not really a lie."

Quick as a flash, Markie said, "It's a game!"

Now, Ross is great at games. His eyes lit up. "I bet I'll win," he said. He put his dogs on their leads.

His chance was coming because we all saw Dean drifting down the street, heading for Ross's house. We all looked away.

I said softly to Ross, "Now, Ross, Dean will try to make you see him. He might even hit you, or kick you, but you've got to make him think he isn't there at all. OK?"

Greg told him, "Remember, the one who pretends the best, wins."

Ross grinned. "I'll win," he said as if he knew for sure he would.

We all waited. What was Dean going to do? Which one of us was he going to punch or thump? I closed my eyes. Would it be me?

In the end, we didn't have to worry at all. Dean didn't attack any of us. Because we weren't the only ones who could see Dean.

The dogs could see him.

They not only saw him, they remembered him. Dean, their old enemy. When he was a ghost he had always chased them and kicked them. The dogs took one look at Dean and they barked and yelped and pulled at their leads.

"Get these mutts away from me!" Dean yelled as they tried to jump all over him.

"What on earth are the dogs barking at?" Ross said. I was well impressed.

"They seem really mad about something," Greg said.

"I think they sound angry," I said.

"And when they're angry, Ross, do they bite?" Markie asked. I think he hoped Ross would say "yes".

"They just eat whatever they're angry at," Ross said.

"Even better!" Markie said.

Out of the corner of my eye I could see terror on Dean's face. "Get them off me!" he yelled. We ignored him.

"I'm not going to be able to hold onto them much longer," Ross said.

Right at that moment the dogs broke free. With a wild jump they were after Dean. He screamed as one of them snapped at his drainpipe trousers. Another took a bite at his backside. "Wait till I get that daft old woman!" he yelled as he ran. "Those boys can't see me at all."

Chapter 5
I'll Put a Spell on You!

Markie was dancing around like a mad thing. "Dean can't get us. We got rid of him once, and we did it again."

He began to sing a rap song. It was almost the same as the song that had got rid of Dean the first time.

"We got that ghost to go too

We got that ghost to go too

We got that ghost, we got that ghost,

We got that ghost to go

TOO!"

Then he jumped up and punched the air.

Ross and I danced and sang it with him.
"We got that ghost to go too,

We got that ghost to go too

We got that ghost, we got that ghost,

We got that ghost to go

TOO!"

Greg wasn't so happy.

"We haven't got rid of him yet," Greg said. "He's gone back to Baggie Maggie. I think we should find out what's happening." He was already running across Ross's garden. We all ran after him. We jumped over Baggie Maggie's fence and her bin bag flowerbeds. We crept up to the kitchen window.

Baggie Maggie was sitting at the table beside Dean, wiping his hand with a brown paper bag. He pushed her away. "Ouch! That's sore. Nothing ever hurt me when I was a ghost."

"Well, you're not a ghost now, my darling boy. So when a dog bites you, it hurts."

"You've done something wrong!" Dean snapped at her. "I must still be a ghost. None of those boys could see me. It's not any fun if they can't see me."

Baggie Maggie put her hands round Dean's face and pressed his cheeks. I wouldn't want anyone to do that. "Does my boy want some fun?"

Dean tried to tell her but her hands were still on his face and his mouth was all squashed up. "Yes, Mum," he mumbled.

"Then it's fun you'll get," Maggie giggled. "But first, you've got to give your old mum a big hug."

Dean turned green at the thought of it. I didn't blame him.

"I wouldn't hug her if you paid me," I whispered.

We all watched in horror as Baggie Maggie crushed Dean in a bear hug. I almost felt sorry for him. Almost, but not quite. He pushed her away from him.

"Right, what are you going to do? And it better be good."

"I'm going to put a spell on *them*," Baggie Maggie said.

"Wha ... wha ... what did she say?" Markie said. His voice was trembling.

Ross shook his head. "She can't put a spell on anybody. She's not a witch."

"There is no such thing as witches," I said. I wanted that to be true, so much.

"We didn't believe in ghosts, until Dean came along," Greg said, and that made us all tremble.

We all stared in at the window. It was getting dark outside, but we couldn't move. The wind began to howl and Maggie's paper bags began to blow around her garden like ghosts. Baggie Maggie began to dance around the kitchen, and wave her arms about. Her plastic bags floated round her. She began to moan. Dean took a step back. I think he thought she was going to be sick all over him.

Then she started singing. At least, I think it was singing.

"Plastic bags, poly bags, where you put

your lolly bags,

Cash bags, sick bags, getting on your wick

bags,

Bags for a beggar and bags for a king,

Bags with the power to do anything."

"I don't think that'll ever get to Number One in the charts," Markie said.

"Ssh!" I told him.

Every bag in Maggie's house seemed to come alive. The bags lying on her floor, the bags hanging on her door, the bags pinned to the wall, the bags waving in the hall. Even her bin bag began to move.

"It's only the wind that's making them do that," Ross said.

None of us believed him. Something very funny was happening.

Maggie was still singing.

"Help me make them sorry, use all the

powers you've got.

Turn them from the boys they are, to

everything they're not."

"That's a daft spell," I said. "What does it mean?"

Then Baggie Maggie threw a handful of something in the air. Something that scattered around the room like magic dust.

"It might be someone's ashes," Markie said.

"Rubbish!" Ross said. "She got it out of her Hoover bag."

He might just have been right. At that very moment, Dean started to sneeze.

The room was suddenly filled with green smoke. Baggie Maggie began to laugh like a mad hyena. Dean stopped sneezing and he began to giggle. She grabbed his arm and they both started dancing and singing around the kitchen.

"What do you think is going to happen now, Greg?"

We all looked at him for an answer. The smartest boy in the school. He had to know.

He shook his head. "I've got a really bad feeling about this."

Chapter 6
All Change

Next day strange things began to happen.

Markie walked into the playground and I had to look twice to make sure it was really him. Now, Markie always has the coolest haircuts in the school. He's famous for it. Today, his hair was all flat and kind of parted in the middle.

"What happened to your hair?" I asked.

He patted it. "I know, it must be that new shampoo my mum got. It's rubbish." He tried to push his hair this way and that but it just stayed flat on his head. "I look stupid." He looked at his reflection in one of the windows. He checked himself out. I had to agree with him. He did look stupid.

And it wasn't just me.

Sunna and her pals saw him too. Sunna used to be Markie's girlfriend but they'd fallen out.

"Markie! What have you done with your hair?" The girls were giggling and nudging each other.

Now, most of the girls at school admire Markie. No girl had ever laughed at him before.

Markie spat on his fingers and tried to get his hair to stick up in spikes as if he'd gelled it. It didn't work. His hair fell down flat again, only this time it looked wet.

A gang of boys came over to see what the girls were laughing at. There are some boys in the school who think Markie is full of himself. But, as he told me, he can't help it if he's the best-looking boy in the school.

The boys started laughing at him too.

I wasn't going to stand for that. No one was going to make fun of my best friend. I walked up to one of the boys. Big Billy. He's the biggest, meanest bully in the school. "Stop laughing now, horse face, or you'll be wearing your teeth as a necklace."

Suddenly I was terrified. What had made me say that? And why had I said it to the biggest bully in the school? To make matters worse, now I was grabbing his jacket and pulling him close. I even kicked him on the shins! I would have punched him on the face too if I could have stretched up that far.

"Duncan!" Markie yelled at me. "Are you mad? What are you doing?"

I wanted to yell back, "I don't know. Stop me, please!" But all I did was kick Big Billy again.

It was the first time Big Billy had had anyone attack him. It took him a moment to fight back. When he did I was thrown over the school wall and landed in a bush of nettles.

The headmaster dragged me into his office. "Duncan, you're such a good, well-behaved boy. I don't know what got into you."

I wanted to say, "Sorry, sir." I tried to say, "Sorry, sir." But what I said was, "Shut up, you big fat tub of mush."

The headmaster went red in the face, then green, then blue. In fact, his face turned tartan. "Duncan! What has got into you?"

And that was when I spotted Dean. He was standing behind the headmaster. He was jumping up and down and yelling, "It's working! The daft old bat got it to work! You're turning into everything you're not!"

Chapter 7
Somebody Stop Me!

After that the day just got worse and worse. I was sent back to class. Dean came behind me, dancing. Markie was sitting in class bent over his desk. He was working hard. Markie, working! I'd never seen such a thing before. His hair was parted in the middle and his trousers were pulled high, almost up to his chin.

He looked up at me. "Help me, Duncan!" he said in a squeaky voice. "I can't stop working. I've even asked for extra homework. And listen to the way I talk. It's a squeak. I'm turning into a geek."

Then he caught sight of Dean behind me. He jumped to his feet. "It's all your fault." Markie made a lunge at Dean and tripped over his shoelaces. He fell flat on the floor. "As soon as I finish my homework, I'm going to thump you," he squealed.

Dean only laughed.

Greg helped Markie to his feet. "You think you've got problems," he said. "I failed my maths test." He was upset. "Me? The smartest boy in school! I just couldn't work out what two and eight were."

Greg didn't just fail his maths test. He failed in English as well. Before he even started the test. He couldn't remember how to spell his own name. Greg had turned into the thickest boy in the school. Markie's voice was getting squeakier every minute. He kept yanking his trousers up high and sniffing and he couldn't stop asking for more homework. Sunna kept making a joke of the way he was talking. So I landed a punch on Sunna's nose. "Somebody stop me!" I yelled.

Somebody did. Sunna. She grabbed me by the hair and she and her pals pushed me into a cupboard and locked the door. That was when I saw Dean again. He was in the cupboard too. "This is so much fun," he laughed. "I wish you could see your face."

Markie and Greg rescued me. Every second that went by Markie's voice was getting higher and higher. And Greg was getting more and more stupid, and I wanted to fight with everyone. As soon as I was out of the cupboard, Big Billy and his pals started laughing at Markie and Greg. I wasn't having that. So I jumped on them and started punching them all.

"Don't do it, Duncan, let the boys pick on us if they want," Markie squealed. He slapped his hand across his mouth to shut himself up. "Somebody stop me!"

Greg and Markie dragged me out of school with the boys and the girls all running after us. Ross was at the gates. He was chasing his dogs, throwing stones at them. Ross! Who couldn't hurt a fly!

I pulled away from my friends. "I'm not running away from anyone," I yelled. I turned to face one of the boys behind us and started another fight. Greg tried to hold me back but he fell down beside me.

Markie kept shouting, "No fighting, please!"

Somebody shouted, "Stop your squeaking!" They dragged him down with us. The dogs jumped on us too. All they wanted was to get away from Ross. Ross jumped after them.

And all the time there was Dean. He stood watching us and laughing himself silly.

It took the headmaster, two teachers and the lollipop lady to break up the fight. Me and Markie and Greg and Ross were all dragged in front of the headmaster. My second time that day!

"What's got into you boys?"

Markie yanked his trousers up even higher and squeaked, "It wasn't our fault, sir."

Ross shouted, "It was those dogs that did it. I hate dogs!"

"There was too many of them, sir," Greg said. "There must have been at least five."

"There was ten, Greg," I told him.

"I can't count more than five now, Duncan." He was ready to cry.

I saw Dean at the window again. We all did.

"And you, Duncan," the head said. "What have you got to say for yourself?"

I looked round at my friends. "Stop me, boys," I begged.

"Stop what, Duncan?" the headmaster asked.

"Stop me. Please." Because I knew what I was about to do. But my friends couldn't stop me. I knew they couldn't.

"Stop what?" the headmaster asked again.

I gave up. "This, sir." And I picked up the vase of flowers on his desk and emptied it over his head.

Chapter 8
Help!

"There's got to be a way to get rid of him!"

That was all I could say as we walked home. My mum was going to kill me when I got there. The head had already rung her. He had shouted into the phone, with flowers and leaves still hanging off his head.

I looked at Greg. "Can't you think of anything?"

"Me?" Greg said. "I'm thick. I even had to put this on to remind me where I live." And he held out his wrist. He was wearing a wrist-band with his address printed on it.

"I'm going to set the cats on Dean," Ross sneered. "Then I'm going to set my dogs on the cats. Then I'll set the horses on the dogs … and that way we'll get rid of all the animals in the world. I hate animals."

"I think we should talk about all this and perhaps then we can come up with a sensible solution which is non-violent." That was Markie. His voice was getting squeakier by the minute.

"Oh, shut up!" we all shouted.

"Thank you," Markie said. "I needed that." He stared at his reflection in a shop window. He looked like a real geek. "Help me, somebody! Somebody stop me!"

Just then we saw that Ross was getting ready to throw a brick at a cat. "Somebody stop me!" he was shouting.

At that moment, Greg walked into a lamp-post he hadn't seen. "Somebody stop me!" he yelled.

I put out my leg and tripped up a little boy who was running out of the shop. "Somebody stop me!" I shouted.

And all the time Dean was walking behind us and laughing himself silly. "This is even better than being a ghost! I never had this much fun when I was dead."

Everything was his fault. He had turned me into a bully. Well, fine! Now I was going to bully him. I threw myself at him with a wild cry. I landed a punch on his face and Dean didn't like that one bit.

He fell back on the ground and rubbed his head. "I'll make you sorry you did that," he said.

"You already have!" I shouted.

The other boys held me back. "He's not worth it, Duncan."

I had never felt so angry. Me, Duncan, the boy who never lost his temper. I looked around at my friends. Markie, the best-looking boy in the school (I know because he told me), had turned into a real geek. Greg, the smartest boy in the school, had to count on his fingers. And Ross, the kindest boy you could ever meet, was trying to knock a bird out of its nest with a brick. There had to be some way to stop this. There just had to be.

"I'm going to Baggie Maggie! Get her to put a spell on you!"

I knew that was a daft thing to say. Baggie Maggie adored Dean. Nothing would make her put a spell on him.

Dean knew that too. So he really began to laugh. He laughed so hard I thought his drainpipe trousers were going to split.

"Baggie Maggie put a spell on me?" he giggled. "That daft old bat thinks I'm wonderful. All I have to do is call her Mum, and tell her I like her. Like her? She makes

me sick. I've seen better-looking frogs than Baggie Maggie. She smells like one of her paper bags that's been filled with dirty nappies. Yuk!" He pretended to be sick on the ground.

I was shocked. "That's terrible. That poor old woman loves you!"

Dean didn't care about that. "And her cooking? The dead mice tasted better! And the daft old devil thinks I like her! In her dreams!"

Just then there was a rustle beside us as if someone had just dropped a whole load of plastic bags. We all looked, and there was Baggie Maggie coming out of the shop.

She'd heard everything Dean had said.

Chapter 9
The Perfect Servant

Dean turned to see what we were all looking at. His face went three shades of green when he saw Baggie Maggie standing there. Today she was wearing a bag on her head which said, MERRY CHRISTMAS. I could see there was a tear in her eye. For the first time I felt sorry for Baggie Maggie. She had treated Dean as if he was her own son, and this was the thanks she was getting.

Dean started to splutter. "Eh, I was, eh, only kidding. I was kidding them on. Honest … Mum? I think you're wonderful, Mum. I think you're the most lovely woman in the world, Mum." He kept saying "Mum" over and over, hoping it would soften her up. It didn't. There was no way Maggie was going to believe anything Dean said now.

"Think you can fool old Maggie, do you?"

Dean looked scared. He began to back away from her. "What are you going to do?"

Baggie Maggie cackled like a witch. "Let me see …" She turned to us. "Maybe you boys can think of something?"

"Don't look at me," Greg said. "I'm thick."

"Turn him into a snake," I said. "That won't be too hard. He's almost a snake already."

"And I'll get the dogs to eat him," Ross said, then he clamped his hand over his mouth. "I didn't mean that. Honest."

"Let's do nothing violent," Markie squeaked.

"Make him as stupid as I am!" Greg said.

And that gave me the perfect idea.

"Yes, Maggie. Why don't you do to him, what you did to us ... make him everything he's not."

Ross smiled. "Yeah, make him kind to animals."

Dean yelled. "Anything but that!"

Markie grinned. "Turn him into a geek."

Dean yelled again. "Anything but that!"

Maggie laughed so much her paper bag fell over her face. "Brilliant," she mumbled. "First I'll turn you boys back to what you were before. *Then* I'll put a spell on you, Dean, and make your worst nightmare come true."

****

We still see Dean every day when we go to Baggie Maggie's after school. Dean makes the tea for us. He still wears his drainpipe trousers, but now he tucks a bin bag into his belt as an apron. He always wears an apron because he does all the housework for Baggie Maggie. He washes the windows. He dusts and polishes. He brushes the floors. Baggie Maggie says he's the perfect servant. He no longer has the wave in his hair you could surf on. Now, he wears his ginger hair parted in the middle and flattened down with gel.

"I look stupid," he'll shout.

And we agree. He does look stupid.

Ross brings all his dogs to the house with him, and Dean pats them and feeds them and lets them lick all over his face.

"This is killing me!" he'll shout.

"He's wonderful with animals," Maggie says.

He fusses over us at the table. He asks us if we like his cakes. "I made them just for you," he tells us. Then he yells, "I made cakes. I'm in hell! Somebody stop me!"

But he does make good cakes.

The other thing that's happened is that Dean's become very clever. He even helps Greg with his homework. Maggie says she forgot when she made the spell that Dean was as thick as a brick before. Now that he's turned into everything he wasn't, he can do sums with his eyes shut.

Dean still has his moments when he's himself. And that's when he's scary. One day as we were leaving, he came to the door with us and just for a moment he was the old Dean again.

"One day," he said, "Maggie's spell will wear off and you'd better watch out. Because I'll be coming to get you ... one by one."

But we got rid of him before. He can't scare us any more ...

I hope.

Barrington Stoke would like to thank all its readers for commenting on the manuscript before publication and in particular:

Rahul Bagai
Michael Barker
Louise Barrett
Richard Bowser
Jessica Bradford
Jason Clarke
Judith Clarke
Rebecca Crowhurst
John Curtis
Janet Dobney
Shamila Gostelow
Mrs G Hardy
Emma James
Mehul Jesani
Jacob Kamoum

John Lyle
Sachin Malkan
Arash Manshadt
Deborah Marshall
Mrs Alison Martin
Morassa Masudi
Ann McCrorie
Gary Mitchell
Jack Moore
Craig Nelson
Oluwaseun Oladipo
Conor Pearce
Gayathri Sritharan
Mrs Trew
Cameron Young

Become a Consultant!

Would you like to give us feedback on our titles before they are published? Contact us at the email address below – we'd love to hear from you!

info@barringtonstoke.co.uk
www.barringtonstoke.co.uk

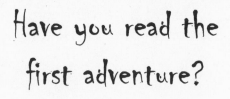

Have you read the first adventure?

Get that Ghost to Go!
by Catherine MacPhail

What would it be like to be haunted by a real ghost? Duncan doesn't know what's hit him when Dean's ghost begins to follow him everywhere. Dean chases dogs and upsets the teachers but no one else can see him. So Duncan gets the blame! How on earth can Duncan and his best friends get that ghost to go?

You can order *Get That Ghost To Go!* directly from our website at www.barringtonstoke.co.uk